KARYA

KARYA

ARAVIND MALAGATTI

Translated from the Kannada by
SUSHEELA PUNITHA

PENGUIN

An imprint of Penguin Random House

HAMISH HAMILTON

USA | Canada | UK | Ireland | Australia
New Zealand | India | South Africa | China

Hamish Hamilton is part of the Penguin Random House group of companies
whose addresses can be found at global.penguinrandomhouse.com

Published by Penguin Random House India Pvt. Ltd
7th Floor, Infinity Tower C, DLF Cyber City,
Gurgaon 122 002, Haryana, India

Penguin
Random House
India

First published in Kannada as *Karya* by Allama Prakashana, Mysore, 1988
This edition published in Hamish Hamilton by Penguin Random House
India 2021

Copyright © Aravind Mallagatti 2021
Translation copyright © Susheela Punitha 2021

ISBN 9780670095780

Typeset in Adobe Garamond Pro by Manipal Technologies Limited, Manipal
Printed at Replika Press Pvt. Ltd, India

www.penguin.co.in

MIX
Paper from
responsible sources
FSC® C016779

KARYA

Wormy Brains and Grey Heads

Countless walked down the length of the street and yet their mouths were locked; silence had swallowed their words. Nevertheless, the sound of their strides could be heard clearly.

This group of more than 200 feet was divided into three.

The first two feet of the leading group belonged to Ghategara Mallappa. He held a stock of cow-dung cakes in his left hand and in his right, he carried the *kullaggi*, the ritual fire amid four burning dung cakes, to perform the third-day rites for the dead person. His expression was solemn as he walked purposefully. The smoke from the smouldering dung cakes swirled about him like a hooded snake, egging him on. Though the white smoke stood out stark against his dark body, it merged with the dun-coloured turban.

Right behind Mallappa was Fakirappa. He held the *kavala mora*—a winnowing tray with bits of boiled meat, bones, brain, tongue and eyes of goat, some roti, savoury snacks like chakkuli and chivuda, a chipped cup of tea, some broken rice and two bottles of medicine. A new piece of white cloth covered them all, fluttering in rhythm with his footsteps. Fakirappa held it down firmly; his face grim.

Those in the second group followed empty-handed. Some were bald, some had had a haircut. Some wore caps; some others, turbans. They walked swinging their arms as if marching off to war, dauntless; muffling a cough so that no one could hear it.

Women made up the third group, their saris covering their heads as well as their mouths. There were more *muthaide*s than widows in this group, and no unmarried girls. Some held on to each other. Some others walked supported by other women on both sides. Their faces looked spent with weeping. Their breath heaved with grief as they walked along. And yet the wretchedness in their eyes seemed to say, 'Let it be; don't weep,' as they walked resolutely towards the graveyard.

Women from the by-lanes stood with mouths slightly open; eyeing them with compassion, talking among themselves:

'It's already been three days since Bangaravva died, isn't it?'

'Yes, don't know how the days have slipped by.'

'That's the way it is with a muthaide's death.'

'Whatever it be, one must be born with such blessings.'

'True, true, she was like a goddess; that woman.'

'And she had a fitting funeral, I heard.'

'Yes. Why, didn't you know?'

'They gave away two bags of jawar.'

'And they tossed coins all along the way, from the home to the graveyard.'

'Yes, it seemed like a shower of rain.'

'Our children brought them home, in their clothes, in their caps.'

'Bangaravva's family is showy.'

'True, there's no one like them among the Machagera community.'

'They stuffed her mouth with gold coins; that's the word going around.'

'*Ayya*, who does all that after a person dies?'

'No one spends as much even when a daughter dies.'

'One should be that blessed.'

'*Avva*, they say, if you drape a corpse with a grand sari, if you fill her mouth with gold, the Adavi Chonchas will dig up the body and steal everything. Is that true?'

'Why only them? Even magicians may steal the bones.'

'Ayya, what kind of talk is that? No mourning is enough for Bangaravva; no ritual is enough for Bangaravva.'

'Bangaravva is Bangaravva! She's gold like her name.'

'She was chaste, like Ganga.'

'When we went to the fields, she'd fill our bags with grain until we cried, "Enough! Enough!"'

'And when we went to her house for alms with a sling bag slung over the shoulder, did she give us any less? "Why have you come with a *hadlagi*? Why didn't you bring a proper bag, a *jolgi*?" she'd say.'

'Shiva has his eyes on such people; she should've lived longer.'

'But one must be blessed to die as a muthaide.'

'Why would anyone look at a widow's face?'

'But it would rain even if such women were widows.'

'She had four sons like tigers and yet she was like stone.'

'*Ayyo,* I spoke to her just a few days ago.'

'And she spoke so warmly.'

'What a death, O God! You snatched her away in a flash.'

'Couldn't he take old women like us, that *Kurasalya*?'

'Today looks like the third day ritual.'

'Yes, look how many people have gathered.'

'Ayya, you should've seen on the day of the funeral. A sea of people! A large circle of relatives.'

'Who died?'

'Machagera Shivappa's wife, I hear.'

'Her eldest daughter couldn't come for the funeral, I heard.'

'Yes, looks as if she's here for the third day *karya*.'

'Look! That fight-a-cock, Gangavva is with them.'

'Whatever be the ill-feelings, one should go. In the end, what will we take with us, after all?'

'Who's holding the burning dung cake? Isn't that Mallya?'

'Yes, but why is *he* holding it?'

'His father must've gone elsewhere, that bastard.'

'Let him be. Why d'you think of such things at such a time?'

The women from the slums stood in the lanes and talked among themselves as they watched the crowd going towards the graveyard for the karya. The mourners went past the settlements of the Dora, Samagara, Katagara and Muslim communities. The Holeyas and Madigas had visited her slum before they had set out, weeping their grief. The women kept talking even after the people on their way to the grave to perform the death rites disappeared from sight. Their tongues wagged to a continuous rhythm, missing a beat here and there.

Funereal Journey of the Living Dead

The men on the way to the karya stopped suddenly at the boundary stone as they reached the limits of the village. The women in the third group were still some distance away.

A buffalo was swimming in a tank within the bounds of the village. Akkavva, from among the women going to the karya, stopped in her tracks to gawk at it, even as she handed over her pitcher of water to another. Her face, screwed tight with weeping, filled out suddenly like a pumpkin, beaming. It was three months since she had lost that buffalo while grazing it and she had been fretting. Now, she recognized it by the ornamental tip-covers on its horns. For a moment, she thought of the dead Bangaravva and turned back to get her buffalo. Who knows if it would come home on its own or not? Some of

7

the women who had seen her, turned up their noses at her and walked on.

The men had the, 'ask them to hurry up' expression, aimed at no one in particular but as if surely meant for the one particular group that was lingering. Just that no one said it aloud. The women stepped up their pace. The woman who had taken the pot from Akkavva walked briskly, ahead of them all. The men stood facing the village, with their back to the boundary stone. Once water was poured over the stone, they continued on their way facing the graveyard. All of men had the same solemn expressions. The women followed them, matching their strides.

That was when they removed the fresh white cloth covering the kavala mora. Their faces perked up to see the crows that had followed them, thanks to the aroma.

The wind picked up as soon as they crossed the village. Even before this, smoke from the smouldering kullaggi in Mallappa's right hand had touched the dung cakes in his left; turning some of them too to ash. Once they crossed the boundary stone, the front wind caused the smoking kullaggi to catch fire. To keep his fingers from burning, Mallappa kept moving them to safer spots on the *berani* and screaming for fresh ones, '*Ei*, this is hot! Give me some more.'

Their feet swallowed the distance. All at once, the men opened their mouths; they murmured:

'Ei, don't let the kullaggi fall.'

'It shouldn't touch the ground.'

'It's bad luck if it does.'

'Don't let it fall. Come what may. Control the blaze; don't let it burn so bright.'

Some even tried to put it down. But the flame would not be subdued. A boy picked up a fistful of mud to throw at it.

'Ei, into whose mouth are you trying to throw mud?' shouted Shivappa, Bangaravva's husband. The fingers of the fist that held the mud loosened slowly, on their own. Mud dribbled through as flour from a flourmill, all along the way. They were getting closer to the graveyard. Mallayya tried his best to press the dung cakes against one another to control the fire. But the headwind was too strong.

'Chikkappa, *kullu*!' he shouted for dry dung cakes to his uncle, Chandappa.

His uncle had fallen behind. All eyes turned towards him even as their strides quickened. Chandappa, feeling their eyes, darted towards Mallappa.

'Why, didn't you bring enough?' he asked.

'I did . . . but they're over . . . *You* said you'd bring some, didn't you?'

'I? When did I say that?'

Mallappa went cold. He broke out in a sweat. His mouth went dry.

'What do we do now?

'We'll do whatever. But don't drop it.'

'Chikkappa?'

'Chikkappa, he says, Chikkappa,' Chandappa muttered to himself. And then to the men around, 'Ei, go and gather some kullu drying in the fields.'

Even before he could finish, a few youngsters jumped the fence and entered the field with a standing crop. But none of them returned. Everyone scolded Mallappa. Everyone cautioned him from letting the ritual fire touch the ground. More than anyone else, Chandappa kept at it. Mallappa's hands trembled as the heat touched them.

'Chikkappa—at least fetch a flat stone to place under the burning cakes,' Mallappa screamed but his uncle showed no concern. He was waiting for those who had gone to get some dry dung cakes from the field. When Shivappa brought a flat stone to help Mallappa, he shouted at him, 'Why, do you want to snuff out your progeny by blocking the fire with stone?'

'Not just his offspring,' added another elder, 'Looks as if he wants to burn down his whole house.' Then Shivappa remembered his only son, Suryakantha, the fruit of many vows to many gods. He was already nearly chest-high. Not willing to lose him, Shivappa did not let the stone fall gently to the ground; he dropped it with a thud. It fell on his big toe and . . . blood flowed.

Mallappa, caught amid the words of caution from everyone, tried his best to put out the fire with his hands but in vain. Already the hair on his hands was singed.

The flame was trying to burn them. He gasped, helpless. Tears ran down his cheeks. And, finally, when the burning dung cake scorched his iron-like hands, he screamed and let go of the kullaggi! He looked at his hands, sobbing. They were covered with blisters. He looked around at the others. Their looks were like knives. Those who had gone to fetch dry dung returned with some. They looked from Mallappa to the burning kullu on the ground. The ash was blown away by the wind and sparks of fire flew from them, happy to have won!

Everyone stood silent for a while. The wind had lost its gusto. All those who had come to attend the karya felt the whole world had come to a standstill. They had even forgotten they were alive.

All this happened in just a few moments.

* * *

Then everyone came alive like clockwork dolls, as if they had been rewound. Suddenly, they surrounded Mallappa; some raised their brows like questions; some frowned, furious; some seemed calm, like a full stop. Only a few showed concern, but they were of no account. Words shot out like bullets:

'Look what ruin you've wrought!'

'Are you happy now?'

'You've spoilt everything.'

'If you'd only held on to it for a while, what would you have lost?'

Mallappa had no answers to their questions; he showed them his blistered palms, two to three blisters on each hand. Though the men were at a loss for words for a while, they said the same things over and over again. The women took another stand.

'Maybe the third day ritual has to happen here.'

'If that happens it's like ash in everyone's mouth.'

'Elders can handle that burning pain. How can a youngster bear it?'

'True. What a thing to happen when we wanted to finish the rites and go home early.'

Shivappa glared in the direction from where the comments were coming. Chandappa sat on his haunches and, gathering the kullaggi into a pile, said:

'Elders should be here for these things.'

Others added their comments:

'What else can you expect from such ignorant people?'

'He withstood at least so much because he's strong.'

'If it had been anyone else . . . '

Ammanna of the Dora community butted in.

'So, Chandappa, what do we do now?'

'If you ask me, what can I say? Whatever the Panchas decides. It's for the council of elders to deliver justice, isn't it?'

'What do you say, Shivappa?'

'Let's go by what the Panchas say.'

Shivappa was already on his haunches. Now he spoke with his eyes on the ground.

'Then, where's that Channappa?'

'Which Channappa?' asked Babanna.

'That harelipped Channappa. Who else?'

Babanna felt bad he had opened his mouth at all; that reply stung him. He recovered slowly and replied to Dora Ammanna.

'Looks like he isn't here.'

'But he looked as if he was coming when we set out.'

No one replied to that.

Ammanna grumbled to himself, 'These people have no sense of time. They try to be elders doing big things. All they do is to shit big. Is this any time to go?' And turning to the hot-headed youngster, Babanna, he said, 'Run! See if he's in the toddy shop by the pond. Bring him here!'

That daring Ammanna had forgotten he himself was tipsy. Babanna had to listen to him as an elder; there was no other way. Even as he left, he heard the others.

'Ei, run!'

'And don't *you* get stuck there.'

'Come back soon.'

After the Burial

Babanna did not run, however much the others urged him on. He only changed his pace slightly. He had a reason for doing this. On returning home after the burial, Seerappa of the Korava community had brought back the ten rupees paid to him for playing the *sanadi* at the funeral.

'Why have you given me only this much when you've given the others so much more?' he had asked, returning it.

'This is part of the ritual. You should've asked at the grave. Should you ask here at home? The saying is true: those who have lost weep for the dead, those who have carried the body, cry for payment,' was the reply he had received.

Hearing this rough argument, Babanna had taken the drunken Seerappa aside and soothed him with some money from his own pocket. By the time he returned, the

Machagara Panchas who had gathered in front of Shivappa's *Myagina Mane,* the Upper House, had dispersed. Only Shivappa's son, Suryakantha, was there, seated on a ledge, his head between his knees.

'Where's everyone?' Babanna asked, touching Suryakantha's head.

'They got the money. What else will they do? They went to the toddy shop to roll on the floor,' he said raising his head slowly, sneering.

'To the toddy store? Who gave them the money?' Babanna settled down beside Suryakantha who carried on in the same vein.

'Even as you went that way with Seerappa, the relatives who had come for the burial threw some coins here on this same platform. Chandappa gathered all that money and gave it to my uncle, Mallappa *mavaiyya* and said, "Here's two five-rupee notes and some twelve paise coins." Ghategara Mallappa brought jaggery and fried gram and served them on a piece of gunny. Everyone made a show of munching on them before rinsing their mouths. They made tea with the leftover jaggery and served it.'

'Ah, they've performed the *isabayi,*' put in Babbanna.

'What's isabayi?'

'It's a ritual after the burial . . . But where did they get the money to drink?'

'They had decided on something when Vaala Lachmavva died, hadn't they?' Suryakantha continued, 'That the bereaved should not light the kitchen fire for three days after the burial? And so, after they rinsed their mouths, other families brought them roti, dhal and broken rice, whatever they had. But some said, "Let's not do this. It's like taking alms. Let's collect money instead and cook for them." And everyone had agreed to it, hadn't they?'

'Lachmavva's is a long story. She had that lump on the back of her neck; on the right side. And there's a saying: if one has a growth on the right side, his wealth will never dry out. What irony! She died of starvation.'

'And so, they collected money,' Suryakantha carried on, ignoring the intrusion. 'But, unexpectedly, some women brought us the food they had cooked. And then, there was an outcry, "Ei! The women have brought food." "Who asked them to? Had anyone told the women what we had decided on?" "Weren't they told? They must have been." "What's the point in telling one or two? Everyone should be told." When the ruckus died down, they decided it was not proper to return the food. They kept it and, with the money collected for the purpose, they went to the toddy shop.'

'During weddings, they get drunk to celebrate,' Babanna said, butting in, 'And even death becomes a reason for such revelry.'

Getting up to go, he said to Suryakantha, 'It's already late tonight. Hope they'll be sober. We'll have to feed the birds before dawn. That's the ritual for the third day.'

Suryakantha, Shivappa's youngest child and only son, was still a boy, studying at an ashram in Bijapur. He did not know much about traditional practices.

Babanna knew very well that the men had gone to get country liquor sold near the potters' kiln. Upset that they had gone without him, even though he had taken on his share of the responsibilities, he went to a toddy shop and got drunk.

The men who had collected the money and gone to get drunk were aware which of the women at home would drink. And so, two cans of liquor were sent to them. The inebriated fell weeping on Shivappa's shoulder, comforting him on his wife's death. No one could understand the other in that drunken state. Shivappa too had drunk a little and was sunk in his own thoughts. Though the men staggered homeward like the tossing of a buffalo's tail, no one lost his way; their feet were that well-trained.

It was two hours past sunrise. Some were sitting up. Some were sipping tea. Suryakantha went around inviting everyone to set out for the rites of the third day.

When Babanna reached Shivappa's house, Myagina Mane, only a few people had assembled there, all of them sober. Shivappa asked Babanna to get the others. Babanna did that obediently, going from one home to the other, asking people to hurry up.

The women had not touched the liquor sent to them the previous day. And so, the cans stood in the backyard, full to the brim. When harelipped Channappa went there to fetch something, he spotted the cans. He lifted the cloth covering them, had a few pegs, came outside and signalled to the others. One by one, the others too went until they had turned the cans and mugs upside down. Then they spoke to one another with their eyes.

'Very sour.'

'Yesterday's stuff. That's why.'

'Too much of powder.'

'It's settled at the bottom.'

'Is there any more?'

'No, it's empty!'

When Babanna returned, it was not long before the smell of toddy hit him. But just to be sure, he asked, 'What's this? The sun has barely risen and the badshah of liquor seems to have descended on all of you.'

'If you had come when there was some, you too would've got a little but you've come after it's over . . .' replied harelipped Channappa.

Babanna went to the backyard. It was clear that the drinking was over and there was no toddy left. The can and mugs were sleeping. He had not got his free drink either the previous day or even this morning. Furious, he was waiting to pounce on someone and walked briskly towards the liquor shop. He had decided to settle scores with Channappa himself if he got a chance.

* * *

Swaateheraka Channappa was the eldest of the elders in the Machagara community. A drunkard known for his short temper, the nickname, harelipped was a title he had earned!

He had had a great life as a youngster. Once he was drunk and was cutting a piece of hide with a *reppige* in his front yard when the tanner, Dora Ammanna, had come to ask for payment for the hide he had supplied. Channappa's father was splintering ambari wood to add it to the bin in which the hide was being processed into leather. Ammanna stood talking to Channappa's father. He referred to the break-up of Akkavva's engagement.

'How can there be an alliance between the Samagaras and the Machegaras?' was Channappa's stand.

'What's the difference between you and them? Both are cobbler communities working with hide,' said Ammanna. 'You could've gone on with the betrothal.'

Channappa pounced on Ammanna, spoiling for a fight. '*You* give *your* daughter in marriage if you want. Why should we?' His upper lip was cut in the brawl. And from that day he came to be known as Swaateheraka Channappa.

Harelipped Channappa was among those who were going for the karya on the third day. But he slipped away while they were crossing the boundary stone of the village. When he reached the toddy shop, his eyes fell on Gidda Basappa, the dead Bangaravva's elder brother, who had just arrived from another village, Khembavi. Both of them went in together.

Babanna had come in an angry mood, looking for Channappa. But his fury mellowed as he smelt the toddy from a distance. When he stood in front of the shop, he saw Basappa, inebriated.

'What, *mava*? When did you come?' Babanna said, in greeting.

'Just now,' Basappa replied, reaching out to another coconut shell on the shelf, meant for Dalits. He stuck a finger in the hole in the shell and called out to the owner, 'Pour another dram here, *appa*.'

As soon as he got his measure of liquor, he asked Babanna to sit, and handed him the shell of toddy.

'Why didn't you come to the burial?' asked Babanna, sipping with his eyes closed, 'Had you gone elsewhere, with fruits and coconut for something auspicious?'

'My sister was like a goddess. I couldn't bring myself to see her face. I'd gone to Ranganapete instead.'

'O, to do with leather? That woman ran away, that *baddarabadaki* . . . The funeral was very grand.'

Basappa ordered another dram for Babanna. Babanna was delirious with joy. They put their arms around each other's shoulders and wept. Babanna had quite forgotten that he had come looking for harelipped Channappa. When Channappa returned from urinating and sat down to comfort them, Babanna began to tackle him about cheating him out of the two sessions of free drinks, like dragging a bull to the pond.

Yamanappa and Hanumantha, part of the group of men going to the third day ritual, came looking for Babanna who had been sent to bring the others. They were upset to see them all in the toddy-shop, sitting and drinking.

'You were asked to bring the rest. Did you too settle down to drink with them?' said Yamunappa.

Babanna shrugged off his stupor, scratching his bum in embarrassment.

Hanumantha told them in detail about the burning dung cakes falling to the ground.

'What! Did the kullaggi fall? Where? How? Why?' Babanna was breathless.

'Very close to the graveyard. Near the potter Kallappa's gravestone.'

'How did he drop it? This shouldn't have happened, it's inauspicious!' swore Gidda Basappa.

Hanumantha and Yamunappa cooled down when they were served a few pegs. Basappa paid for the coconut shells. And all of them swaggered out of the tavern murmuring to themselves as if deep in thought.

'Bangaravva was a like a goddess. Che, this shouldn't have happened at her death,' was the general trend of their gibberish.

Though they had crossed the boundary stone and reached potter Kallappa's gravestone, no one was in sight. Only one person seemed to be out there, in the hazy distance.

'Are they here or have they gone back?' asked Gidda Basappa.

'How can they go away, after dropping fire on the muthaidhe's head?' answered harelipped Channappa.

'What shall we do now, *kaka*?' That was Hanumantha.

'Whatever's to be done rests with the elders,' said Channappa. 'They've desecrated the kavala mora.'

Gidda Basappa nodded. 'Ayyo!' he moaned, 'I didn't get to see my sister's face. Did I come to see this desecration? How inauspicious!'

Hanumantha and Yamanappa comforted him as they walked him on. No one was aware of who was holding on to whom. But all of them were on the right track.

Split in the Ghategara Household

After Babanna had headed towards the toddy-shop to look for the others, the people on their way to the karya were exhausted standing; they sat about in small groups. But they would not let Fakirappa either sit or put down the kavala mora, the tray of food for the dead.

'Don't sit. You'll have to pay a fine if you do,' they warned him.

'Once the kavala mora is lifted, it should be put down only on the grave, not anywhere else,' they cited custom. And so, Fakirappa had to remain standing while the others sat around.

It was already midday. With the sun overhead, those who were drunk felt dizzy. They talked among themselves.

'Anyway, why did you let Mallappa carry the simmering kullaggi for the ritual?'

'I had gone to get his father, Varaga Dasaratha. He's not well. He's been in bed for quite some time now. And so, he . . . '

'But the lad is still young; he doesn't know much about these things.'

'He's training to be a wrestler.'

'Even when Lachmavva died, Varaga pleaded, "I can't do this anymore. I've been carrying the dung cakes for the third day ritual. Please give it to someone else." But will Shivappanna listen? "Ei, let all the jobs of Ghategaras be with your family," he insisted. And now this has happened to get them into trouble.'

'No, when I went to call Varaga, he said, "I don't feel up to it. Take Mallya. He must be in the farmhouse." When I went there, I found him with that woman. He was unclean but he didn't even wash himself when he came to carry the kullaggi. I kept quiet. Why should I make a fuss in front of the others?'

'Really? Who's that woman?'

At that very moment, they stood up saying, '*Oi*, those who'd gone to call the others for the karya have returned.' But the other bit of news was smouldering in whispers among them.

Those who returned and those who had been resting gathered where Fakirappa was standing.

As they stood around the pile of burning dung cakes meant for the ritual, Dora Ammanna addressed them as elders, 'Whatever has happened has happened. It has slipped through our fingers. That Mallappa didn't know any better; he let fall the sacred fire.'

'Ei, Ammanna, what do you know?' Harelipped Channappa stepped forward, still heady with drink, 'Is he a boy? That father of two! The wrong he's done is wrong.'

'Today's the third day ceremony, the feeding of birds,' added Gidda Basappa. 'This is like desecrating the kavala mora. Bangaramma was like a goddess—my *thangi*—she's one among our forebears now . . . Should we feed our ancestors that?'

'Yes, yes, you're right,' nodded the others.

'From the day I was born until today, when I'm grey, I've never seen nor heard of anything like this,' sighed Ammanna, stepping back. 'Whatever it be, the third day ritual has to be performed on the third day. Let's do whatever your Machagara Panchas decides.'

This was a new experience for everyone.

'Who wants this job of a Ghategara?' protested Mallappa, hurt with listening to sarcastic comments. 'I don't want it. I don't want to do it.'

'Yes, let him not do it,' agreed some from the gathering. Chandappa supported them, heartily.

He had a reason.

Chandappa was Varaga Dasaratha's younger brother. Dasaratha had many children. And so Chandappa had moved away from the joint-family fearing he would have to share his earnings. Within a few months of moving out he contracted leprosy and had to live on his elder brother's charity though he lived separately. But the people of the village had another story about him:

'He came upon a pot of gold while tilling the field. He didn't want to share it with his elder brother. So, he moved away. Also, he put his hand in the pot without propitiating it first. And so, his finger and toes fell away. Not just that. He hasn't any sons. The brothers divided the treasure between themselves, true, but they can't stand each other.'

Chandappa, did not mind their version. He just smiled; it was a good enough front to hide his leprosy.

Dasaratha had proposed to hand over his duties as Ghategara to Chandappa, when his younger brother had lived with him. The elders too had agreed to it. But when Chandappa lost his fingers and toes, they did not want him as their head. That is why Dasaratha had to continue in his role. And when the old woman, Lachmavva died, Shivappa had said that Dasaratha's son, Mallappa, could take over the responsibilities from him. The elders had also agreed.

Chandappa seethed against Dasaratha and Mallappa; they had deprived him of his position as Ghategara and the earnings that came from it. He wanted to wrest it from them, deviously. And now, he was happy; everything seemed to be falling into place in his favour. He had deliberately not carried the extra dung cakes though he had promised

Mallappa that he would. And now, he was fuming against Mallappa; more than he needed to.

But the men could not come up with an alternative, however long they discussed the matter. Every solution seemed to have a new problem hidden in it. Since they did not have the wisdom to handle the situation on their own, they remembered Buttolli Jangama.

With use, the expression, Buttolli had become mispronounced as Butali. And they had got into the habit of referring to the ascetic with respect, as Butalayyanavaru. The name went well with the kind of a hermit he was. He challenged the saying, 'An ascetic is born after a thousand monkeys die.' No one had crossed the limits of the village and gone to the slums of the lower castes to beg. He was the first person to step into the settlements of the outcastes. 'It is your good fortune to wake up every morning, smear *vibhuthi* on your forehead and look at the face of God,' he said to them, implying that he was the deity. This tantric had hidden the fact that this was his way of earning a livelihood. He became a revolutionary as being the first person to beg food from the Dalits!

And now the men sent Chandappa himself to get this ascetic and awaited their arrival.

Pointless Fuss over a Corpse

For the Veerashaiva ascetics known as Jangamas, some sects of Dalits are the main clientele. In a business without capital, the *panchanga* is their only investment. And the future they forecast from this almanac is their merchandise; never mind that it is repeated, parrot-fashion. People listen to his predictions standing outside the door as if it were the truth from the Vedas; they believe they have no salvation without the Jangamas. The Jangamas also have the practice of dividing up the Dalit settlements among themselves once every two years so that they do not trespass on each other's territory. How did this bond grow between the untouchables and the ascetics? No one knows!

The colony of the Machagaras came under Butalayya's jurisdiction. So, they consulted him, without fail, for every ritual connected with weddings and deaths. The family that sent for him had to pay in cash for the items, like grains and fruit, needed for the ritual *puje*. The articles were considered worthless if the family bought them or provided them from their home. All the items used for worship went into the Jangama's sling-bag. They had to give him some gift-money too.

It was the same during a funeral. After the burial, there was the ritual washing of the Jangama's feet over the head of the dead person; a stone was placed on the head of the grave on which his feet were washed. But before the washing was a ceremony, similar to the proverb, 'The one who beats the drum at a funeral, weeps according to the payment.' So, the more the money, the more the wailing. The Jangama was initially stubborn, venting his ire, faulting the dead until he was suitably mollified with money. Then, he washed his own feet. Only then would the dead attain *mukthi*; those assembled heaved a sigh of relief and those who had eaten dared to burp. Once this was done, the Butalayya made sure he had a bath somewhere before he reached home. Not only after a funeral but after a wedding as well! Such was the connection between the Ayya and the outcastes. And that was why Chandappa was sent to the 'revolutionary' Butalayya's house now.

When the elders saw him returning without Butalayya, they were downcast. And yet they were curious to know why he had not come; they wanted to hear the story from

Chandappa himself. And he was eager to tell the elders. And so, he began:

'I told him everything that happened here. But Butalayya said he would not come. If you ask me, "Why? Why?" What can I say? This food is three days old. The ascetics won't even look at it, let alone eat it.

'But why talk about them? Even our people won't come to look at it, so why talk of him? And then, Butalayya can't receive any gift money during the third day ceremony. Why will he come? This is also the truth.

'But he has told us what's to be done. Fakirappa should not be allowed to take even one step further. He should not let go of the kavala mora. He shouldn't even shift it from one hand to the other.'

We're to put the kullaggi into the same tray and take it back to where the peg was hammered into the wall on the day of the funeral. The tray should be buried there. And then, fresh food has to be cooked. Plenty of it.'

Based on Butalayya's advice and their own take on the situation, the elders prepared to deliver the verdict. But Kallappa thrust a spoke in the wheel.

'Before we arrive at a settlement, let Mallappa tell us why he let the ritual dung cakes drop.'

'All of you saw what happened. Where's the need for me to tell you?' said Mallappa.

'Not about what happened here. Tell us what happened in the farmhouse.'

33

'Farmhouse . . . ? What happened at *the farm* . . . ?'

'Aha, asking us as if you were innocent! I came and woke you up. Don't you remember? You were impure. You touched everything without washing. That's why all this has happened.'

All those waiting for the ritual to be done began to talk among themselves. Kallappa told them everything in detail. The comments from the women supported whatever he said.

'Bangaravva was a virtuous woman. Why would she want such disgusting people to pour milk over her grave? That's why she's done this.'

'They're like cats that close their eyes and drink milk. And he's smart enough to say his hands got burnt carrying those burning dung cakes.'

'Let him do what he pleases and fall into a well. But he should've had a cleansing bath before coming here.'

'She was a god-like person. Would she let anyone defile her?'

No woman spoke aloud. And yet the Panchas heard them. They too felt the women were right. And now it seemed the verdict would take another direction. Even if Mallappa had made a fuss that he had done no such thing, no one would have heard him.

'Whatever it be, we've got to settle it here and now and then talk about other things.'

'What's there to discuss? That was the general consensus,' Dora Ammanna, who had been sitting quiet, stood up and said, 'Yes, whatever it might be, settle the issue right here.'

That the ritual fire had been dropped was a first not only to the Dalits of the Muddhalli slum but for people from other settlements too. And now it was taking a new turn. The elders were confused, as if they had lost their way. Also, they were too drunk to think of a way out. Only Chandappa gloated secretly.

'The Panchas never had to deal with such a problem,' he grumbled.

When he heard Dora Ammanna mention, 'Mallappa . . . farm . . .' he guessed who the woman in question could be and was happy. He vowed in his mind to offer five pairs of coconut and two peeled bananas to Bangaravva's grave if things turned out the way he hoped.

After a while he stood up and said, 'What's there to discuss? Last year, while returning from the pond, the chariot of the goddess Dyamavva had got stuck in front of Shanthagowda, Rudregowda's younger brother. Didn't the goddess enter the Badigera pujari, possessing him to say that the Desai had defiled the temple? Didn't he and the woman pay a fine? The same thing can be done here too.'

There was no need to elaborate on that incident since most of them knew the details. Ammanna did not feel inclined to explain the situation; his sister, Chandravva, was the woman who had slept with Shanthagowda in the temple. And the elders of the village and Rudregowda himself had brought Chandri to the altar of Dyamavva, imposed a penalty and collected it from her.

The elders decided that the woman in question in this incident too had to be brought here and the two be made to pay a fine.

But no one knew as yet who the woman was. When the question was raised, 'Who's the woman?' the answer was a while in coming. When Kallappa was asked, he slipped away, saying, 'The *kusti pahelwan* is the guilty one. He's right here; ask the wrestler.'

Mallappa, looking as if he had the muscle of all the Dalits in the colony, spoke gruffly, 'I've done nothing of that sort.'

Finally, Kallappa spoke up, 'It's Padmavathi, Shanthagowda's second wife.'

Everyone was uneasy, confused. Especially the women; they felt scared to talk about it and yet they belittled him, 'As the father of two children, did you have to do such a thing now?'

But the men were drunk; they had the bravado of men!

'Justice is justice.'

'Why should it be different for different people?'

'What does it matter who it is? The Panchas are the ultimate council. Who can stand against them? One has to come when asked to come and go when asked to go. Even a king is but a son to his mother, isn't he?'

The Machagara Panchas made such decisive statements with a drunken daring. They were not clear in their minds about whom they were talking. They knew what it was to get involved with the Gowda's family. They knew very well what had happened to the Badigera pujari who had spoken on behalf of the goddess when the chariot got stuck in front of Shanthagowda. Having forgotten that incident, they now believed the Machagara Panchas had immense authority. That was because they had excommunicated the arrogant Machagara Parasappa, prevented marriage alliances with his family and banned him from attending funerals and other rituals. The elders now presumed they had enormous powers. They pronounced their verdict:

'The decision of the Panchas is firm and clear. Whoever it be, everyone is equal in the sight of law. First, the woman must be summoned and penalty levied and collected from both the guilty.

'Second, Mallappa must surrender his position as Ghategara. Only then should the kullaggi and the kavala mora be taken home and new ones provided for the ritual to be resumed.'

It was also decided that no one was to stir from the place until the first two conditions were fulfilled.

It was around three to four in the afternoon by the time everything was finalized. Some of the men who could afford it, had gone for a drink, with permission from the elders to pee. The women stood about whining, listening to their

37

drunken bravado. They were worried about the children at home. But they had to conform to tradition too.

'This ritual is for the third day; it has to be done today. It cannot be put forward,' grumbled Sangavva, an old lady. 'What decisions are you taking in your drunken state? The children at home are dying of hunger. By the time the kavala mora is taken home and a new one brought, it will be night.'

'Let it be night or day, so what? Anyway, we'll be doing the rituals on the third day, won't we?' said harelipped Channappa.

But when it came to sending someone to the Gowda's house to bring Padmavathi, everyone backed out. Finally, they decided to send Kenchappa, inebriated as he was. He worked for the Gowda; had he a tail, he would have been the Gowda's dog.

Shivappa, Bangaravva's husband, sat through it all like a mute bull. Even if he did try to get in a word edgewise, Channappa stopped him with, 'See Shivappa, this is the Panchas's responsibility. Since we've entrusted the matter to them, you keep quiet. If you open your mouth, we'll go away and then, you do whatever you want to.'

Shivappa shut up, intimidated. To his son, Suryakantha, all this seemed strange. To some who stood about watching, this was a kind of entertainment; they intruded with pointless questions. Some others furthered their own ends with their suggestions.

Fakirappa began to moan. His legs were aching from standing with the kavala mora.

'You're holding the mora as a relative. You can't put it down. Bear with it or else you'll have the same fate as Mallappa,' said some. He glared at them.

Fakirappa was already a bit unsteady on one foot. He was a strange kind of a drunkard. If other men beat their wives when drunk, he beat up his children. His wife was the no-nonsense type, hard-working. Once when he tried to beat her, she had hit him so hard that he was hurt at the hip and walked with a limp since then. And now the pain had returned.

Shivappa went back to the village and woke up a relative asking him to take Babanna and Kenchappa to the toddy shop. Both of them went happily. In situations connected with death, toddy is tastier than food!

Broken Pot and Leaking Issues

Inebriated as he was, Kenchappa went to bring Shanthagowda and returned in the same stupor. It was already quite late in the day but no one had made the effort to go and find out why Kenchappa was so long in coming. When he did come, Kenchappa announced drunkenly, 'Master's not at home, they said.'

'What if he's not at home. You should've asked *her* to come,' said harelipped Channappa, slightly tipsy himself.

'How can that woman come when the elders are not at home?'

'Does everything happen only when the elders are at home?'

'Whatever. The elders have to be there.'

'Were there any elders when she lay in the farm?'

The suggestive comments flew back and forth. By then, some of the men were emerging from their stupor. They were beginning to be aware that they may have gone beyond the bounds of propriety in summoning the Gowda's wife to pay a penalty.

'But we're only following rules; we haven't crossed the mark,' was their only comfort. It was a matter of honouring the council's decision. No man could disrespect it. 'If we flout our own rules, what will people say? That the Panchas of Muddenahalli could not resolve an issue.' Some of the elders were most concerned.

Expecting the master's return that evening, they made Fakirappa stand with the food-tray in front of the burnt dung cakes and waited. After a while, Suryakantha himself went to the Gowda's house; the master was not in, really.

The women began to murmur again. The crows that had been waiting for the food in the tray had flown away. Now the women raised their voices.

'You couldn't feed the birds on the third day; you couldn't feed the bereaved.'

'How long are we to sit here waiting? We're going.'

'What else can we do? Children at home might be crying to be fed.'

'They seek justice, they say, justice. All of them are drunk.'

'What do *you* lose? You go and drink and come here and sit, saying you'll dispense justice. Can we do what you do?'

'Instead of weeping over the corpse, we have to weep over you now.'

Shivappa sat with his head bent. He was upset to hear the women. If the others were smarting too, they did not have the courage to speak. Shivappa spoke to harelipped Channappa and Ammanna of the Dora community.

'The time for the third day ritual is running out. Even if the Gowda returns home now, it's unlikely that he'll come here. Let's go back. We can do the third day ceremony tomorrow.'

'Look here, Shivappa,' said Dora Ammanna, 'It's a matter of maintaining prestige. Not yours, not mine, but that of the Panchas. Your duty is to do whatever the elders decree. Now that they have taken a decision, you have to respect it. Let my life or yours go today . . . Or else, why did we take all this trouble?'

'Yes, Shivappa,' Channappa added his bit. 'It's not a big deal to go back home. But it's the matter of upholding the verdict.'

'So then, are you saying that our children have to die of hunger at home?' Murugappa burst out in fury; he had held it in for too long.

'Ei, shut up! The elders will decide on that too,' said someone sitting next to him.

'Then, let's send away the women,' suggested Shivappa. 'What will they do, sitting here?'

The elders talked among themselves. And then, Chandappa stood up and said to them, 'Look, you elders, with your permission, let the women go home. What do you say?'

'Yes, let them,' said the elders, one and all. Though he was a leper, Chandappa thought of himself as the Ghategara and did what the Ghategara should have done in giving the women permission to go home.

'Fine. Come when you do,' said the women. They had been waiting for this. They only felt sorry for Fakirappa as they walked away.

Fakirappa was moaning but no one came forward to comfort him. It was a tricky situation; neither could they spit it out nor could they swallow it. His face was shrivelled like a roasted brinjal.

The news had already spread all over Muddenahalli. And since they were sitting outside the village, passers-by stopped to find out what was happening before they went on. People from nearby villages like Hulagabala, Vadageri, Nagarabatte, Hulluru, Mudnala, Shirola, Kuntoji, Basarakoda, Nidagundi and Erajheri, chewed on the news with their betel leaves and nut. And the two who danced on their tongues and were caught among their teeth were the Gowda's second wife, Padmavathi and the *pahelwan*, Mallappa.

* * *

There was neither grief nor solemnity among the women who had left the ritual half-way through. Among them, Sangana Basavva was the only one who had become a strikingly different person. She was Fakirappa's wife. She had been keeping quiet while she was among the men. But now her mouth was set free to spit venom all the way back home.

' . . . She died, that blessed woman; she reached heaven. In her name, these people are trying to kill others. They keep saying, "Stand. Stand." How long can he stand? And that too, on one leg. Is he a man or a buffalo? Is it our fault that we happen to be related by marriage to the dead person? Was it wrong for him to hold the kavala mora? Why're you asking me to shut up, *akka*? They've taken on the affairs of the village and decided to dispense justice in their drunken state. Justice, indeed, justice.'

With one stare she swallowed up the woman who was trying to pacify her.

Her voice grew softer as they neared the village.

As they neared the village, they could see lanterns. The slum-dwellers had been curious to know what the verdict was but no one had the courage to probe since they were Dalits. They presumed the matter was resolved and the people had returned after pouring the ritual milk on the grave.

The first house on the rise after the entry-gate to the village was the front-door of the Myagina Mane, the

45

upper house. And that is how Shivappa's family were known; the people of the upper house. Also, it had another special feature: this was the only house built of mud and stone among all the houses in the Dalit colony. The rest were thatched huts of woven date palm smeared with dung. The first few houses near the entrance belonged to the Katagara, Korava and Dora communities of Dalits. And then a few houses of the Machagaras and Samagaras. Lastly, those of the Dakkaligas of the Madiga community and then, the Holeyas. This is how the outcastes lived, in hierarchic groups.

Even as the women crossed the settlement of the Katagaras, they were asked if they had brought greens. When they said, 'No,' the people were certain the third day ritual was not yet completed. When they reached their area, they could see that old women and those who had recently delivered babies had lit the lamps. Children were catching frogs by their legs and tossing them out of the houses. Other homes were dark, like graves.

No fire was lit in Myagina Mane and the homes of the close relatives of the dead. It was three days and three nights since the kitchen fires were lit in these homes. Smoke wafted easily out of other homes. Even if people from such homes brought food to the ones who could not cook, they would not eat; it would be like eating poison. And most of them were women. Some who had cooked, fasted. How could they have the heart to eat when their menfolk were starving? Some others, of course, fasted like monkeys who fast because they have nothing to eat, anyway.

Snakes on a New Moon Night

Mallappa's father, Varaga Dasaratha, the bed-ridden elder of the Ghategaras, had heard the news from his bed. He was waiting eagerly for someone to come and take him there. He had been ignored; he was hurt. He passed the night as if on a bed of thorns.

He had been waiting for sunrise. As soon as he saw the first rays, he went and sat on a stone bench, dragging his feet. He watched the children walking back and forth. But he could not see any familiar face among them who would listen to him. Of course, he knew where the men would be at this early hour in the morning! Nevertheless, he looked, first this way, and then, that . . . hoping.

The children were in front of a toddy shop near the marketplace, holding small basins. Yellappa, a toddy tapper of the Eligara community was taking down loads of freshly brewed toddy delivered on horseback. It was customary to give some toddy as alms before it was emptied into bins from the leather bags. The Dalits firmly believed it was their primary duty to go wherever whatever was distributed as alms. And this was the only true God-given wisdom they passed on to their progeny. So generally, at daybreak, their children went to the leather sacs filled with liquor, received the bounty, drank half of it and carried the rest home. But today, they drank all of it and danced their way home beating a rhythm on the empty bowls.

'What is it to them what happens to others?' thought Dasaratha, looking at them, 'It's like the proverb: While the old woman worries about her son-in-law, her daughter worries about her paramour. What does it matter to them what happens to whom? After all, they're children, aren't they? When grown-ups get drunk and loll on the floor, why fault the children?' He took one of the boys and went towards the graveyard.

The toddy shop beside the pond was closed and barred. 'Why is it locked?' he wondered, 'Perhaps, it's been closed since yesterday. Would something else have happened in the village? Could there be a *kala numbri*? A curfew? None of our people would've had anything to drink then. I can have a quick talk with them.' He dragged his feet, chatting with the boy.

As he neared the group waiting to perform the third day ritual, there was only one man standing! One or two sat with their heads between their knees and some others slept, curled up like fetuses. As he came closer, he saw Fakirappa propped up on the forked limb of a tree. His feet looked swollen. His knees were bandaged and the cloth tied to the fork to prevent him from collapsing. Even his hand with the food-tray was supported by another forked branch. And he was made to rest with his back to the village, facing the graveyard. Fakirappa began to weep when he saw Dasaratha.

'*Kaaka*, I'm dying! I'm dying!' he kept repeating. Dasaratha signalled to him that he should remove the cloth from his knees and sit down. Fakirappa shuddered as if he had seen a snake.

'No, kaaka, no! The Panchas have threaten to fine me even if I move my foot.'

'Who said so? As long as you don't lay the kavala mora on the ground.'

Fakirappa had no reply. Dasaratha wiped his tears and comforted him.

Hanumantha and Yamunappa, who had been sitting with their heads bent got up and came to stand beside Dasaratha. Suryakantha had gone to ease himself and now he came and stood near Fakirappa. He had wiped himself with a stone; there was no water anywhere.

'What d'you think you're doing? Why're you doing this?' Dasaratha asked them, looking at Suryakantha.

'Not we, only they,' the boys replied.

Hanumantha and Yamunappa were still slightly tipsy. What with the drink and lack of sleep, their eyes were red and sticky. Suryakantha looked sober though he too had had some liquor. His eyes were red. So was the eastern sky.

'Have you been drinking fermented dhaaru at this early hour?' asked Dasaratha.

'No, only fresh sendi from the date palm.'

'Is everyone dead drunk?'

'Yes, after the womenfolk left, they just let go.'

'They even went to the toddy shop.'

'But it was closed.'

'Even those from the Dora and Samagara communities had come. They went that way,' Suryakantha provided added information.

'Why will they stay? They'll have to starve if they do, won't they?'

There was silence for a while. Then, Varaga Dasaratha himself broke it.

'From where did they get the sendi, then?' he wondered aloud.

'You know potter Kallappa's gravestone, don't you? Where they pour sendi . . .' When Suryakanatha began, Dasaratha remembered the story suddenly:

Potter Kallappa was a terrible drunkard. They had buried him in the same graveyard. When they were laying a road, they had to destroy some of the graves. But when they came to Kallappa's, their pickaxe and crowbar were broken and they went down with chills and fever. So, they swerved the road around the grave. But, whenever they brought liquor to Muddenahalli from Vadageri and Hulagabala, the bullock carts turned turtle. Even when they brought it on a horse, camel or bullock, the animals could not cross the tombstone. Thus, the practice of pouring a little sendi on the stone had begun. Who knows when this story began? Only, the gravestone was black with all the liquor, like these people!

'Ah! Yes, and then?' Dasaratha asked Suryakantha.

The place was strewn with drunkards hugging the ground. They would not have awakened even if shaken. Dasaratha had to wait until they got up. He sat down.

Suryakantha had been shivering through the night and had gone to sleep at dawn. He did not know what had happened. Hanumantha took over from him. He was known for his narration of folktales and now he told Dasaratha what had happened the previous night with suitable frills.

'What shall I say, kaka? The night was as cold as cold could be. It was dark too, being a new moon night. We wanted to drink a little and sleep off but we couldn't get any country liquor . . . thorny shrubs were all around us . . . chirping crickets, humming insects . . . Any sound was scary; we were close to the graveyard. At that point we heard someone sobbing bitterly. As it is, we were afraid of ghosts. Our hands and feet went cold. Some may have even wet themselves. We covered ourselves with our strips of cloth and lay down. The crying grew louder and seemed to come nearer.

"'Ei, the weeping is right from here," said Yamunappa.'

"'Shut up!" I said, and the crying grew louder.'

Hearing this, not just Suryakantha but even the elder Dasaratha felt scared. Yamunappa listened, open-mouthed, as if he had not seen or heard what was being narrated. The lad who had brought Dasaratha had gone back, frightened. Hanumantha continued.

'As the weeping grew louder, I lifted the wrap and peeped. A ghost right in front of me! And then I heard a voice, "My hands and feet have gone numb! I'm dying." That's when I pulled down the cloth covering me and saw Fakirappa *mava* crying. And then we massaged his hands and feet. We held him up awhile, supporting him. Then we looked at one another. We could hardly see our faces. But we were sure there were just the three of us. The others had bought some liquor and lit a fire and were sitting around it. Some others were loitering about. That's when I shouted out to Fakirappa, "Kaka, hand me the kavala mora, I'll stand with it for a while. No one can make out in the darkness of a new moon night. You sit and rest for some time." But will he listen? I even spoke to him as one would speak to a parrot, "Listen, Kaka, I'll give it back to you even as dawn breaks. You can stand with it then." But he would not listen.

'"No, she was a like goddess. I can't cheat her," he said. He says that and he cries. What can I do, tell me? Even if they had asked us to stand with it, how long could we have done it? And that too, we had become like starving dogs . . .' Hanumantha paused for a while, looked at Yamunappa through the corner of his eyes, swallowed his spit and continued with a smile.

'And then Fakirappa wept that his waist was hurting. We massaged his waist.

'"If only I could get something to lean on," he said. We looked around. There were no sticks around. There were trees, of course, but no axe to cut a forked branch. What else could we do? We looked for a neem tree to break a branch but this Yamunappa, said, "Ei, that potter Kallappa's a ghost, sitting on that tree," and we had no guts to go anywhere near it. We went to those who were warming themselves by the fire. All of them were dozing. All except Mallappa and Babanna; they were talking. We explained the situation to them.

'"Ei, get lost! How can a ghost be there on the neem tree?" said Mallappa. "I myself would've gone and broken a branch for you but what can I do? My hands are blistered."'

At that moment, Dasaratha felt a wrench in his guts, as if someone had branded him. He had heard about the blisters. Mallappa may have done wrong but he was his son, after all, wasn't he? He stood up interrupting Hanumantha, 'Where is he?'

'He's sleeping,' said Yamunappa. All of them came together near Mallappa. He was sleeping with both his palms spread out. Dasaratha wept softly; he did not want to wake up his son. After a while, they went and sat to a side.

Early in the morning, those who were on their way to sell milk and curds from the neighbouring villages, stopped a while as they went past, talking among themselves.

Hanumantha continued with his story:

' . . . and then, Mallappa said, "Come on, everybody, I'll stand there. You climb the tree and cut some branches." And he went ahead of us. I climbed the neem and brought down some branches and stuck them near Fakirappa so he could rest on them. That gave him some relief. It helped him to lean against them.

'We lit a fire and sat around it. We were bored.

'"I'll go home, see my father and come back," said Mallappa.

'"*Ei*, don't. The elders have asked you not to leave this place," said Babanna. He went after him even when he went to pee.

'We were drowsy. That's when I said, "Listen, I'll tell you a story. It's a king's story . . . his wife was friendly with the mahout of the elephant. He used to sing very well. One day she was late in coming to him. He caned her . . . The Raja saw him and hit her later with a flower in the presence of the royal court. She fainted . . . "' Even as Hanumantha was narrating that story, Dasaratha let his mind wander and when he returned to the present, Hanumantha was still talking away.

'... in the distant graveyard, kaka, we could see the glow of a burning stick.

'"Le, that looks like the dancing devil," said Yamunappa.

'"Yes, it does, doesn't it?" added Babanna. We sat huddled, terrified. The burning torch seemed to come towards us. My heart nearly stopped beating. We stood up. The torch went out and vanished! Then we heard voices, speaking in Urdu . . .

'"Hey, wake up! Are you still sleeping? We're here, at the grave of the potter, Kallappa." And then we could make out the voice: It was Nabi's. We guessed they had stopped the cart at Kallappa's grave to pour some palm toddy over it. We were starving. None of us had any money to buy some toddy. We went towards them, nevertheless, to ask for a drink.

'"But this isn't any free liquor to be given away," he said.

'"We'll pay you later. We're like starving dogs; we haven't eaten for three days."

'"OK, pay me when you can," said that shorty, Nabi. "Only, don't give it to me in front of that toddy-tapper, Yellappa." He got the oilskin bag down from the horse and poured out the toddy into our cupped hands . . . we drank and drank with no count of how much we drank. We brought some for Fakirappa too. Nabi kept pouring toddy into our cupped hands until we were gasping for breath.'

'Anyway, you cheated Yellappa, all of you,' said Dasaratha.

'Why only he? Two have been cheated,' said Babanna, sarcastically. In a way, Bangaravva was cheated too. Fakirappa should have been fasting but now he has broken his fast, cheating the dead woman.

'And then, you know what happened, kaka,' Hanumantha continued. Words hidden in their bellies tumbled out, one by one.

'We should've done what the priest told us to do.'

'It was all Kallappa's doing?'

'He may have seen Mallappa with Gowda's wife but why should he bring it up here?'

'That whore's son! The pahelwan.'

'But Kallappa could never beat Mallappa . . . he was waiting for a chance . . . '

'What a stupid thing to do!'

What began as a grumble gathered fury against Kallappa; everyone swore against him, everyone cursed him.

And they praised Mallappa.

' . . . He endured the pain only because he happened to be a wrestler. Would anyone else have let their hands get burnt that way?'

'Why talk about anyone else? Even this very Kallyya would have dropped the kullaggi right at the village.'

They continued to talk among themselves, sitting down. As they stopped, Yamunappa butted in.

'Nabisaheb had an axe. We cut down a forked branch and set it up to support Fakirappa.'

Generation Gap and Respect for Elders

Varaga Dasaratha stared at the faces of those who had gathered around him. All of them belonged to the Machagara community and no other. The elders of a few other castes were arriving now. Each one who came protested that he had not gone home.

Fakirappa rested on the support provided by the branch of the neem tree. Some of the men massaged his hands and legs from time to time. He was not as weepy as he was the previous night.

'Wonder if it's because he resting on that stick or because of the liquor and tea he's had,' muttered some among themselves. Fakirappa hoped for some respite, now that Dasaratha had come.

'What, Fakirappa? Have you eaten from the kavala mora meant for the dead? The night was dark, thanks to the new moon,' someone asked. Fakirappa's eyes dwelt immediately on the food-tray he was holding. The egg, liver, lungs, tongue and brain of the goat looked half-eaten! The bones, the savoury snacks, broken rice, bananas and medicine were untouched. There was some liquor left in the liquor bottle but it looked lighter in colour, as if diluted with water. Fakirappa looked at all that.

'No! I haven't eaten any of this,' he said.

'So, did I eat all that?' said someone else.

Fakirappa was silent.

'If you were hungry, you should've told us. We would've got you some food from home,' said Ammanna. Fakirappa protested that he had not eaten any of it. Those who were sitting about came over to take a look at the winnowing tray. They passed rude comments as they went by. Fakirappa teared up again. There were not many to speak on his behalf. Those assembled said whatever they pleased.

'How could he eat like that, being as important to the ritual as he is? And he says he didn't, pretending to be innocent. The tray was in his hands.'

'Ei, a demon may have come and eaten the food, without his knowledge.'

'Ask him if he had some drink early in the morning. He must've munched on some and then eaten it all thinking he's eating from his plate.'

'If he says he hasn't eaten, shouldn't he know who else could have?'

How much ever Fakirappa insisted that he had not eaten and he did not know who had, the blame rested squarely on his shoulders. Dasaratha tried his best to plead on his behalf but failed.

Chandappa always held that a penalty had to be paid for everything; either for a commission or for an omission. Even now he insisted that the elders had to levy a five rupee fine on Fakirappa. Two of Fakirappa's close relatives pleaded and fought on his behalf; nothing worked. Shivappa tried to bring some compromise but they pushed him away. No one cared for Dasaratha's efforts, anyway.

By now, Fakirappa had peed a few times in the *valli* wrapped around his waist; people had to hold their breath as they walked by. He had not eaten since the day Bangaravva had died and so he had felt no need to expel anything but now, when he heard all that talk about a fine, he felt a vague stirring in his guts.

'This is the right moment to bend the iron while it is hot,' thought Ghategara Dasaratha. Already quite a few of the crowd were sitting up, what with the heat of the rising sun. The others were waking up. Suryakantha had been sent to get some tea dust and sugar; he had returned. They made black tea on an open fire sunk in the ground.

The men had drunk palm toddy before sleeping and so their eyes were stuck with goop. They woke up and stirred about. They noticed the elder Ghategara Dasaratha, but not many of them showed any respect. Even the few who did, did it more as a formality.

No one seemed to feel the need for water to wash their faces. They sipped their tea and talked casually as they gathered around Dasaratha who sat with Fakirappa. Fakirappa too had his tea. No one asked why the tea was black; they lived dark lives anyway.

Yamunappa had been restless while the trial was on. Dasaratha had sent Hanumantha and Suryakantha to his house after Hanumantha had narrated his story, saying, 'We'll come as soon as this is settled. Meanwhile, go and get ready to dig a pit and prepare another kavala mora for Bangaravva.' Now, Yamunappa sat quiet, wanting to be rid of all this bother. He was the only one who was with Fakirappa the previous night. He was scared he would be blamed for eating the food in the kavala mora.

Dasaratha lost his temper; no one had respected him as a Ghategara. He had been sidelined.

'People have lost their respect for elders,' he shouted, 'You've been discussing this issue since last night, right up to this morning. Couldn't you have come to see if I were alive or dead? Did you think an old man deserves respect only from his immediate family? It's only because I can't walk about that I said I wouldn't be a Ghategara carrying the kullaggi for the karya. Did I say I wouldn't be in the council of the elders to dispense justice here?'

Everyone was quiet for a while. No one was prepared to talk back. Dasaratha of Muddenahalli was well-known among the Dalits in the neighbouring villages as 'one who dispensed justice with a sword hanging over the victim's head'. But now, he had lost that respect because his son, Mallappa, had desecrated the rites of the third day by dropping the dung cakes. Even those who wanted to say something, thought twice.

'It's been a day and a night,' Dasaratha continued. 'You made this man rest on the fork of a branch as you would a she-buffalo in labour . . . Can't you see his feet swelling up?'

'We made him stand as the guru told us to,' said a voice from the gathering, 'What? Would the elders have made him stand that way deliberately?'

'Look! Would the guru have known you'd take a whole day and night to sort out this issue? He would've suggested it as a stop-gap arrangement, that's all.'

'No, he's asked him not to move a step forward.'

'Yes, that's true. They've said he's not to move from there,' said someone else.

'True, he's not to move. And he's not to put the kavala mora on the ground . . . But did anyone say he was not to sit down? It's okay as long as he doesn't keep the food-tray down . . . ,' clarified Dasaratha.

'How can that be? Can a sacrificial buffalo be slaughtered lying down because it could not stand? What are you saying? Have you no respect for what the Panchas have decided?

Are they crazy? Is this the way justice is dispensed?' The one who went on this way, breathlessly, was Chandappa, Varaga Dasaratha's own brother.

Dasaratha was stupefied to see his younger brother standing up to him and speaking against him this way. He could not make out why Chandappa was putting him down, by referring to the Panchas in every line of his argument. What could he say when his own brother was arguing against him? Dasaratha was dumbfounded. He asked the permission of the elders to leave and left without waiting for it, taking Yamunappa with him.

The elders were shocked to see the brothers arguing.

'Chandappa's sense of justice is straightforward,' said some of them, praising his cutting stand. The youngsters did not quite like a leper becoming their leader and yet it seemed that his line of argument, favouring the elders, could make him one.

'Whether he be brother or father, justice is justice,' said Chandappa, and instead of stopping at that, he added, 'What arrogance! He left without waiting for the council's permission to leave.'

Pahelwan Mallappa had been stifling his fury at seeing his father insulted.

'Who are *you* to give him permission?' He now pounced on his uncle, clutching his shirt and raising his hand to slap him. The rest of the crowd caught hold of him and separated them. The blisters had burst on Mallappa's palm.

He looked at them for a moment. Then, picking the green scab of medicinal herbs, he stared at Chandappa.

'I know your arrogance,' he growled, plucking some fresh hatharaki leaves, crushing and smearing them on the palm.

Mallappa was already seething with anger and now with the raw skin smarting, he hissed like a snake clenching his teeth. The others tried to pacify him.

'As it is, he's putrid with that illness. And besides, he's hell-bent on becoming the Ghategara. Who'll give the leper the position?'

'*Le,* get lost! Am I asking you for any favour? The deaf, the lame, the blind rule the country. Duryodhana's father was blind. Hm, he's trying to preach ethics to me!' Chandappa had only spouted what had been dinned into his head at the gym for wrestlers. His tongue had been trained at the Gowda's gym but his head was not clear about its implications.

'Ei, Chandappa, shut up! Why're you growing your tail?' the others said to him, 'Your elder brother did ask for permission to leave; he's an elder too.' They stopped the discussion right there.

Chandappa gnashed his teeth in frustration. 'I won't let this be,' he said to himself, 'I must see how it ends.'

The news of their 'meting out justice' became a joke around the village. People found excuses to walk by casually, stopping to have a look.

But while some made light of it, some others took it seriously too. Fear began to settle in the pit of their bellies: When would the next flare-up be? People who were cowed down until now were raising their heads claiming equal justice for all. How could that be? How far would Rudregowda listen to his younger brother, Shanthagowda, in this matter? Even as the serpent raises its hood, the spear is ready to strike it. We should not be caught in the cross-fire.

They slunk away quietly without even talking about the issue.

A Patchwork Coverlet and a
Bundle of Rags

Shanthagowda arrived at Muddenahalli before his elder brother, Rudregowda. Both the men were contrary in temperament to what their names implied. Rudregowda was gentle and amiable while Shanthagowda was just the opposite; fiery and temperamental.

Shanthagowda heard about the event even as he entered the village. He was depressed as he stepped into his house. After a while, he came out with a gun and a belt of cartridges and headed out with two servants. The servants shivered on seeing his fury. They walked behind him with hands to their chests like dogs with tails between their legs. Though they had expected something like this, though they now followed him in silence, their hearts thumped. They felt Mallappa's life was at stake.

Shanthagowda went straight to the farmhouse, looked around fuming, hitting the ground with the butt of his gun. He was not grinding his teeth against Mallappa and Kallappa as the people thought, but against Chandappa. The master-plan to provide fewer dung cakes to Mallappa and make him drop the ritual fire was not Chandappa's; it was actually Shanthagowda's. He had had two reasons for teaching Chandappa this ploy.

Chandappa had complained to him about the likelihood of his nephew, Mallappa, becoming the Ghategara when the position was rightfully his as Dasaratha's younger brother.

'Please see that the post comes to me somehow or the other,' he had pleaded, 'Ask your elder brother to speak to Shivappa on my behalf.'

'You're a leper. It won't help to put in a word,' Shanthagowda had said and taught him a way of undercutting Mallappa's role as the bearer of the ritual dung cakes. And now it looked as if Chandappa had dropped a stone on his own legs.

Shanthagowda had a grouse against Varaga Dasaratha too; he sported a moustache as impressive as his own. He was so furious that he had sent for Dasaratha as well as the barber, Mallappa, and asked him to shave it off in front of him. But Mallappa of the Nayadara barber caste did not take even one step forward.

'Gowdre, he's below my waist; of a lower caste. How can I touch him?' he had said when Shanthagowda roared in fury.

'What if he's higher or lower? Shave him, you rascal!'

Mallappa began to slink away.

'Hand him the razor, let him shave it off himself.'

Mallappa tossed the knife at Dasaratha and stood aside, relieved.

Dasaratha had cared for his moustache more than for his life.

'*Ayyoppa!* My mouth is deformed,' he bawled while being whipped, 'I've grown this moustache only to hide it. It's not a lie . . . That's why everyone calls me varaga . . . varaga.'

'Oho! Your lips are crooked and so you've grown a moustache, have you? Why, are you thinking of getting married again? Will you cut it off or should I cut off the other lip for you?'

Dasaratha nicked himself twice while cutting one side of his moustache. He was sent home as he was shaving off the other side.

Dasaratha had hardened his heart after this incident. He grew the same luxuriant moustache and went about. He did not respond even when Shanthagowda sent for him.

The Gowda was lying in wait to break his spirit. That was a reason, and then there was his son, Mallappa.

Mallappa was a good wrestler but his guru was a mystery to the villagers as well as to Shanthagowda. Until recently, the wrestler from Shanthagowda's gym had been winning all the bouts but, at the goddess Dyamavva's fair, when the wrestler was about to raise his hand as the winner, Mallappa had challenged him to a bout. Mallappa was sent back humiliated for being of a lower caste. His very masculinity was questioned and the wrestler had started a fight with him.

But what began as a fight ended as a bout. A revenue collector and a police inspector who had come from elsewhere to watch the wrestling matches interfered and arranged for a contest between the two. And the winner was Mallappa. Not just that, he also received a cash prize from them and was carried on the shoulders of his fans in a procession. Since then, Shanthagowda had been grinding his teeth against Mallappa trying to keep him from the ring. He wanted him as his servant but that did not work. He could only get him as the night watchman in his elder brother, Rudregowda's farm. In trying to remove one thorn in the Mallappa issue, he seemed to have got another thorn in his side.

Apart from these two reasons, Shanthagowda nursed a general grouse against Mallappa. And this incident seemed like digging up soft earth with a hoe after a few showers.

Besides, Chandappa too was like a trapped animal. Gowda now spewed fire on that same Chandappa.

Machagara Kenchappa was still tipsy when he reached the farmhouse; he was sent to bring Gowda and his wife Padmavathi. And anyone coming to the house from the council was directed to the farmhouse. They had sent him as soon as they heard that Gowda was home. Now, Kenchappa was scared to go to the farmhouse and, when he saw Shanthagowda, he wet his dhoti. He ran to him and fell at his feet, weeping.

'*Appa*, my father . . . you're like a God . . . They've laid a baseless blame on your family . . . I'm a poor man. It's not my fault . . . I've come because they sent me . . . No, I haven't come for them . . . I've come as a servant of your house.'

Even as he said this, he received two kicks and a jab from the butt of the gun. His lay like a dog with his head bleeding while Gowda shouted at him,

'Sons of whores! What guts! The slippers you make have better value than you. How dare you bring *our* names into your Panchas? Who are you? Who are we? What's your worth? What's the respect we command? Don't you know . . . ?

'You mother fuckers! You sons of whores! You useless bastards! Have you come this far? Like the saying goes, "A slap from a slipper to the god of the Samagaras." I know what to do with you people and how. Get lost, you son of a bitch . . .' Gowda had kicked Kencha again.

'Decide on your verdict within an hour or else I'll chop off your heads like that of ripening corn. Justice, indeed, justice… Can there be one for all?'

Kenchappa walked away with bleeding head and torn clothes. Gowda sent his spy, Nana, immediately after him to find out how far the council of the Machagaras had progressed, and how.

* * *

Nana returned, almost running.

'*Dhanyaare*,' he called out to his master, 'get on your horse right away. Hurry. The news is bad,' and, helping his master on to his horse and running beside it, he provided an update.

'Dhanyaare, when Kencha stood before their council, all battered and beaten, some of the members did get scared . . . He repeated all that you had said, I think . . . Then they really froze with fear. *Abah*, and the verdict! Unmentionable!'

'Look at that . . . ! That dog, Chandappa was trained in our gym . . . And now that he wants to make Mallya eat mud, it looks like he wants to sell us.'

'The council has made Chandappa their spokesman, Dhanyaare, I think they're very happy that you didn't attend their Panchas meeting; neither you nor Padmavva. Chandappa spoke loud and long, knowing there was no one there from our side . . . And then, harelipped Channappa butted in saying, "What are you saying? Listen to what I have to say." It looks as if he too is eyeing the Ghategara's post. "Who appointed you to speak? You leper! You seem to have taken it upon yourself to become an elder here. Who'll let you?" A great argument broke out at this point but Chandappa held his ground . . . He's the shadow at your feet, after all, isn't he?

'Listen, Dhanya, here's the decision of the elders:

'Mallappa has to give up the Ghategara's post; he's dropped the ritual fire. Also, he'll have to pay a suitable fine. Second, there's more to come . . . The ritual fire fell because Mallya wasn't chaste. Also, the Gowda didn't attend the council, nor anyone else. So, Mallya will have to pay a fine on behalf of you as well.'

'Oh, what arrogance! He'll pay the fine on *our* behalf too, will he?' Gowda broke in, furious.

'Yes, *Daiva,* even Dora Ammanna was ranting and raving.'

'And what did Mallya say, *maga*?'

'That Mallya's a rogue, Dhanya. He faced his uncle, Chandappa, and said, "What kind of a beggarly justice is this? I haven't slept with anyone. I haven't defiled myself. Sangya may say whatever he pleases. Tomorrow, he'll say you slept with her . . . Will you accept that? Send for her, if you're a man enough. Or let the council summon her. If she accepts your allegations, I'll close my eyes and pay the fine." That's what he said, Dhanya, that son of a bitch.

'He refers to her as "she" does he? They've become insolent, these fellows,' mused Gowda.

Nana continued. 'When Mallya spoke about Chandya not being man enough, he got furious. They got into a fist fight and I slipped away.'

'I'll finish them off, one by one,' said Gowda.

'If you do that, it'll be like stuffing mud into our own mouths, Dhanya. They've left a gold plate filled with water at our threshold. We'll have to wash it clean with ash and take it . . . Say, Mallappa accepts to pay the fine, it will seem as if the allegation is true. We have to see that he refuses to pay and yet justice is meted out. Other things can come later.'

Nana explained the intricacies of the situation; Gowda could see his point.

Nana was shrewd. But quite a talker. He was notorious enough for people in the town to call him a bragging dog. Everyone knew about the 'broom-service' he had received at the settlement of the Madhara community. He had grown into a legend even before he could die.

As they neared the centre of action, a terrible whirlwind arose and swirled about them. Gowda remembered something similar that had happened. He mused:

'These fellows even skin a corpse to make money; they skin it to make slippers . . . And we wear them and wear them out. And even people without the tuft of hair on the head scare us about gods and retribution. It's like offering our heads to the barber. Will our evil deeds return to haunt us . . . ?'

Gowda felt the spirits of the wind laughing the same way, all over again.

Dark Justice. At Last!

But the place did not look like a battlefield, after all.
Everything seemed to have simmered down. Gowda could
see Fakirappa propped up on a stick. Hanumantha and
Suryakantha had already arrived. There were a few women
as well. The council had agreed to Chandappa's suggestion
offered at the very beginning of the discussion. Even as
harelipped Channappa rose as the leader to pronounce
the verdict, Fakirappa fell from the prop on his wife who
was right beside him, massaging his feet. He had fainted.
The sun was a little below overhead, sinking yet blazing.
Fakirappa had been giddy with neither food nor drink to
sustain him. He fainted as soon as he saw Shanthagowda
with a gun.

As soon as he stood up to speak, harelipped Channappa saw Shanthagowda. The others who were sitting about rose to their feet when they saw him. And those who were lying down, weak with hunger, scrambled up as soon as they heard him roar at them. But none had the courage to lift Fakirappa. Even his wife, Sangana Basavva stood up, controlling tears that overwhelmed her.

As Shanthagowda looked at them, from one to another, Mallappa himself came forward looking this way and that for some water. There was some in a pot, meant for tea. He sprinkled it on Fakirappa's face and head.

'You sons of whores!' shouted Shanthagowda, getting down from his horse and handing the reins to Nana, 'Who taught you to dispense justice? You'll bury even the living.' Even as she heard him, Sangana Basavva felt life flowing into her. The tears she had controlled until now streamed down. She ran to him and fell at his feet weeping. Gowda helped her to her feet and walked away. When she came towards her husband, Fakirappa, she saw all the eatables from in the kavala mora strewn about. Mallappa began to fan Fakirappa with the tattered tray. He signalled to Hanumantha and Suryakantha with his eyes and the three of them carried Fakirappa and laid him beneath the shade of a nearby neem tree. Even before making the sick man smell the onion from the mora, Mallappa sent Hanumantha and Suryakantha to the river for some water.

In a while, Nana came over to call Mallappa, even as he was tending to Fakirappa. As Mallappa walked towards the council, Sangana Basavva called him and offered him the cooked brain which she had tied in one end of her sari. Though he was embarrassed to eat something from the tray meant for the birds, he ate it because of the humility with which she offered it to him and also because Nana was watching him. As he was standing up, he saw something fall from the place where she had tucked in the pleats of her sari at her waist.

'This is the eye, for Surappa,' she said tucking the delicacy back into the folds; she had saved it for Suryakantha. Mallappa followed Nana.

The ambience had changed completely by then. Nana and Shanthagowda stood to a side. Chandappa had risen to the post of the leader of the council instead of harelipped Channappa. Smiling, he delivered the verdict on behalf of the council.

'Hear the decision of the Daiva. Firstly, Mallappa should not have dropped the burning dung cakes. He burnt his fingers and so he dropped them. He will have to pay a penalty for it. Also, he will have to give up being the Ghategara . . . '

'I'll pay the fine. I'll give up the leadership,' Mallappa thundered, butting in, 'Will all of you, members of the Daiva, make good my losses?'

No one answered. Chandappa widened his eyes and gulped, and continued with the verdict.

'The ritual of feeding the birds will be tomorrow. Secondly, there is no connection between Gowdru and Mallappa. There's no blame on Ammavaru. This is as true as the sun and the moon.

'Thirdly, since the Machegara council have discussed Gowdru's family in public, every member will have to fall at his feet to beg forgiveness and stitch a left slipper as penalty. This is the final verdict of the Daiva.' Chandappa brought his palms together with respect.

Everyone was silent. The first thought in their minds was, 'Ayyo, what an affront! We could've stitched a pair of slippers for him. At least he could've asked for a slipper for the right foot.' The upper caste people would deem it a disgrace to take money as penalty from cobblers. True. But, did he have to insult them by asking for slippers for his left foot only? But no one spoke aloud.

Shanthagowda mounted his horse and rode away with Nana running behind him.

Gowda was thinking as he was riding, 'Tomorrow, as soon as the ritual of feeding the birds is done, these people are sure to get drunk with the fine Mallappa pays them; both men and women. All their thatched huts should be torched that very night. Not just this village but even the surrounding villages should get to know what will happen if they mess with Gowda.' He instructed Nana.

As soon as Gowda left, the people crowded around Fakirappa. Hanumantha and Suryakantha had brought water from the river by then. But there seemed to be no point in attending to the sick man. They decided to carry him home. No one was in a mind to talk about the verdict. They had reached a point when they were grateful if they could escape with their lives.

Chandappa brought the kavala mora. He swept up the ash from the kullaggi into the food tray. He also gathered the odd bits of food from the tray on to it. The food was stinking, with flies swarming about it. The burden of carrying the tray fell on Bangaravva's elder brother, Gidda Bassappa. Though he trembled at the thought of what had befallen Fakirappa, Basappa took it on, knowing the ritual had to be gone through.

At least, what they called 'justice' was meted out in two days and one night.

The procession set out homewards. Leading it was Gidda Basappa holding the kavala mora with the dung-ash and stale food. Following him were two men carrying Fakirappa. A few others walked along with them. Someone held Kenchappa's arm supporting him. The third group was of the women. There was a fourth group as well now, walking rather unsteadily with no food and only water in their bellies.

Trailing behind all of them was Suryakantha, Bangaravva's son. He carried an empty pot, upturned. He stared straight ahead as he walked. The sun of the day was dying slowly behind him.

A Place of Unending Sorrow

In Fakirappa's house, some from his family were taking care of him.

In Shivappa's house, some others were burying the *hendi kavala*. It was the cow-dung cakes mixed with the food meant for the crows in the graveyard. No one could eat it. Even Bagaravva's favourite food was to be buried where her body had been made to sit before the funeral. Elsewhere, harelipped Channappa was skinning a sheep to prepare the kavala mora again to carry out the ritual the next day.

'Tomorrow makes five days since Bangaravva died,' Channappa grumbled to himself. 'On the fifth day, Bangaravva's face should be embossed on silver as a *hiriyara mukha*; she's now a forebear. Her *mukha*, together with the other mukhas of ancestors and the deities of the family should be carried to the pond, the *ganga sthala*. An elder should carry them on his head in a basket with the puje items. The mukhas and the deities should be washed and worshipped in the presence of the family. The basket should be filled with water after the puje and a piece of camphor should be lit on a betel leaf. The dear ones of the dead should set that leaf with the burning camphor afloat in that water; it will float towards the person who was a favourite of the dead. Then the deities and the hiriyara mukha should be taken home to be placed in the *devara jagali*. That is how Bangarevva should be received on the shelf of the deities as an ancestor of the family. What a misfortune to do the third day ritual on the fifth day. Who knows what else is in store!'

Except for the fireplace in Shivappa's house, all the others were burning stealthily in other homes. Though food was cooked, it did not taste good. 'How can this be tasty when the food for the third day ritual hasn't yet been eaten?' The women worried.

'When will the night give way to day?' The men fretted. Anyway, they heaved sighs of relief as they watched the sun emerge without any mishap.

They had all been waiting for daybreak. Now they gathered in front of Shivappa's house.

They started out again, walking solemnly as they had done on the third day. The country liquors stores must have been impressed to see them!

As per the Gowda's decision, Chandappa, the leper, was the Ghategara. He held the kullaggi now as the head of the community. As Bangaravva's elder brother, Giddi Basappa walked behind him with the kavala mora. Then followed the groups of men and women. All of them walked briskly.

As they neared the pond, they heard that some two people had fallen into it. Everyone was anxious, uneasy. 'What next?' their hearts thudded. They were not yet sure who had died. 'They could be Mallappa and the Gowda's wife, Padmavathi,' they surmised.

As they crossed the pond, they saw some people swimming to retrieve the bodies. They heard the news after they had passed the pond. Those who had died were Rudregowda, Shanthagowda's elder brother, and Varaga Dasaratha, Mallappa's father!

Now everyone had the same question: 'Where's Mallappa?' They had not seen him since the previous night . . . There were murmurs but over-riding the whispers were the footsteps, sure and decisive.

There were only two who knew the answer to the question: One was Kenchappa; he was in bed, ill. The other was Babanna. He was now talking to Hanumantha and Yamunappa, 'When Kenchappa went to Gowda's house to tell them the Panchas had sent for him, the Gowda wasn't at home. Only Padmavva was in. She gave him two rotis to eat and asked him what the matter was. When he narrated the proceedings at the council, she told him, "Tell Mallappa

I'll be at the cave on the Padmavathi hillock. Hurry up and come." With my own ears I've heard Kenchappa passing on her message to Mallappa. That's why he was giving excuses to get away the day before yesterday night: "I'll go and check up on my father . . . I need to pee . . . " She was in the cave. Shanthagowda couldn't find her at home that night. Mallappa too has been missing since yesterday.'

'Stupid people! I told you about this that night, the day before yesterday. Didn't I tell you that story about a queen and a mahout? It was about Mallappa, the wrestler.' Babanna explained.

By then they were near the graveyard. They had already poured water on the boundary stone on the way. They removed the new piece of cloth covering the kavala mora. But crows had been following them even before they could lift the cover. Everyone rejoiced to see the crows; that was a good omen. The breeze was blowing; the dung cakes continued to burn.

People who saw the crows hovering over them, said, 'Good! The food for the dead will reach her fast.' The crows flew beyond them and settled on Bangaravva's grave and a neighbouring grave. Not just that! There were other crows already there and waiting.

Seeing them, both men and women whispered among themselves:

'What a gathering of crows! I haven't seen such a flock ever.'

'See, what a noble lady! A virtuous woman, indeed . . .
Look at the host of friends she has!'

'We're doing the rites of the third day on the fifth
day . . . wondering whether she would accept it or not . . . '

'Look at this, Shivappa? What d'you have to say?'

'Everything is God's will,' said Shivappa, walking on.

As he walked beyond a few graves, Chandappa stopped
in his tracks. Gidda Basappa too did not take a step forward.
Suddenly, the crows flew away creating a ruckus. Everyone
who reached Chandappa stood stock still, stunned.

Bangaravva's body lay outside her grave.

Their mouths were drained with fear; their guts
trembled, eyes widened with the whites showing, until
slowly, one by one, their brains crept back on their own, to
the task on hand, wondering, 'How did this happen? How
could this be? What next? What next . . . ?' It was difficult to
break that silence. The flying crows began to look like owls.

By and by, darkness seemed to cover their eyes.

Any solutions?

Translator's Note

'Fools rush in where angels fear to tread,' said Alexander Pope and I felt its full impact while translating this novella by Aravind Malagatti.

Tackling the regional variety of north Karnataka Kannada, with its mixture of expressions and sayings from Marathi and Urdu, was intimidating, to say the least. It was quite a challenge to transfer the flavour of the colloquial style to create the right ambience. And I could not have done it without the author's elaborate explanations for not just the meaning but also the contextual significance of expressions. For instance, an expression like *kala numbri* is a compound word, with a blend of Urdu and English to mean, 'black number'. But this bit of lexical information does not help us to get at the contextual implications.

Kala numbri means 'curfew', referring to Section 144 of the Criminal Procedure Code as the kala or black number because it prohibits people on the streets during curfew.

Careless editing of the text in Kannada added to the problems. There were some I could correct and some for which I sought clarification from the author. But the scariest was one I did not even recognize as an error until he pointed it out to me! The expression was *mangala upvaasa*, in the last paragraph of the chapter, 'Broken Pot and Leaking Issues'. It is the description of some people fasting. And I had translated it as 'some others fasted for some auspicious reason', considering all kinds of fasting to be propitious. But the expression was meant to be *mangagala upavaasa*. And I had to rewrite the line as, 'Some others , of course, fasted like monkeys who fast because they have nothing to eat, anyway.' The comparison had a subtle undercurrent of irony. Just as monkeys fast only when they get no food, these people fasted always because *they* had none. The omission of that one syllable—*ga*—made all the difference, converting to fact, the gut-wrenching humour typical of the author's style. And I would have missed it if he had not alerted me.

The story is highly symbolic and I had to use interpolations as scaffolding to interpret culture-specific rituals that point towards the deeper significance. In the last chapter, Channappa's musings on the rites connected with the fifth day after death had to be elaborated to highlight the magnitude of the desecration that follows.

After editing the text, Mini Krishnan, my editor, wondered aloud about juxtaposing *Karya* with *Samskara* since both the stories dealt with death rites going awry. And I recalled an insight I gained when I was interviewing U.R. Ananthamurthy in 2012 for the Oxford India Perennials edition of *Samskara*. I had asked him the reason for all the fuss around cremating Naranappa. And he had explained to me the significance of the rituals on the days following the cremation; rituals that involve accepting the dead person as an ancestor. He said, 'When the Brahmins are asked to perform the cremation, they refuse to do it, not because they don't want to dispose of the body: they don't want him as a *pithru*.'

The community was not willing to accept Naranappa as a pithru for he had flouted the tenets of religion. And here, in *Karya*, we have a community eager that 'Bangaravva's face should be embossed on silver as a *hiriya mukha;* she's now a forebear.'

With a juxtaposition of the situation in the two stories, the contrast is obvious: the Brahmin community in *Samskara* does not want to take on the responsibility of cremating Naranappa as they will also have to perform the rites of accepting him as their forefather but the Machegara community in *Karya* grieves that the death rites going awry on the third day after the burial of Bangaravva prevents them from performing the rites of the fifth day honouring her as their ancestor. It is the incipient irony in the similarity that has to be noted: the death rites in both the communities are so stringent and demanding that the men in the two stories cannot think beyond them. Only the women seem capable of seeing a way out for themselves, like Chandri in *Samskara* and Akkavva and Padmavva in this story.

I thank Aravind Malagatti for responding to every mail to clarify my doubts and clear my confusions. I can never thank Mini Krishnan enough for her meticulous editing and for suggesting further explanations to clarify the context.

This was a scary venture, but I am glad I went through it. It has enabled me to see how tough the going can be and how well collaboration can work to ease it.

—Susheela Punitha

Author's Note

The novel *Karya* was published in Kannada in the year 1988. I wrote it after my grandmother passed away in 1985. During her funeral, the kullaggi embers flared up into a blaze and the person carrying it was forced to drop it. The question which started from there, in addition to the previous incidents and experiences, took the form of a candid realistic novel. Since it has been published, *Karya* has been a textbook for some academic courses, and there have also been some critical writings on it.

The credit for this rendition, from bud to blossom till its fragrance reaches the readers goes to Mini Krishnan who introduced me to the new methodology of collaborative online translation. I was surprised to realize that translation can be done this way, all through email, without face-to-face conversation. Mini Krishnan also introduced me to a celebrated translator, Smt. Susheela Punitha. The spirit of the original work has been encompassed in this rendition with no gaps at all due to the unwavering dedication and diligence of Smt. Susheela Punitha. Her efforts in bringing the indigenous words and the native dialogue structure to life in English are truly praise-worthy. To these two women goes the credit of organizing a triangular discussion over the Internet and bringing out the original in the translation in all its beauty. I am greatly indebted to them.

Glossary

Adavi Concha	tribals of North Karnataka
aggi	fire
ayyo/ayyoppa	expression of grief
baddarabadaki	woman with a questionable character
devarajagali	shelf where the deities are placed at home
dharu	fermented liquor
ganga sthala	pond
Ghategara	the head of the community who carries the ritual fire to the graveyard on the third day
hadlagi	strip of cloth tied at the ends and slung over the shoulder as a bag

hatharaki	a medicinal plant
hendi kavala	desecrated cow-dung embers mixed with food
Holageri	slums where Holeyas live
isabai	a cleansing ritual signifying the end of a phase in funeral rites
jangama	an ascetic
jolgi	bag
kala numbri	literally, black number; meaning, curfew; referring to Section 144 of Criminal Procedure Code
kavala mora	Items taken in a winnowing tray to feed the departed by feeding crows during the third day ritual
kulla	cow-dung that has dried naturally into cakes
keri	the slums where the Dalits live
kullaggi	the ritual fire of smoking cow-dung embers taken to the graveyard to perform the third day ritual of the dead
kullu	cow-dung cakes made by spreading dung on walls and dried; used for rituals
kurasalya	a swear word; here, cursing the cruel god
kusti pahelwan	wrestler

lathi	the constable's stick
matha	monastery
Machagara	member of the community of cobblers
mukha	face; here, face of the dead embossed on silver
mukthi	salvation
muthaidhe/sumangali	a married woman whose husband is alive. She is considered auspicious and, therefore, blessed.
Myagina Mane	Upper House, known for its location and also to signify the status of the family
Panchas/panchayat	village council
puje	worship
punya	virtue
sanadi	a wind instrument
sendi	unfermented drink

ALSO AVAILABLE

Phoolsunghi

Pandey Kapil

Translated by Gautam Choubey

'A Bhojpuri classic revived in English'—*Mint*

When Dhelabai, the most popular tawaif (courtesan) of
Muzaffarpur, slights Babu Haliwant Sahay, a powerful
zamindar from Chhapra, he resolves to build a cage that will
trap her forever. Thus, the elusive phoolsunghi is trapped
within the four walls of the Red Mansion. Forgetting the
past, Dhelabai begins a new life of luxury, comfort, and
respect. One day, she hears the soulful voice of Mahendar
Misir and loses her heart to him. Mahendar too feels for her
deeply, but the lovers must bear the brunt of circumstances
and their own actions which repeatedly pull them apart.

The first-ever translation of a Bhojpuri novel into English,
Phoolsunghi transports readers to a forgotten world filled
with mujras (dance of a courtesan) and mehfils (festive
gathering), court cases and counterfeit currency, and the
crashing waves of the River Saryu.

ALSO AVAILABLE

The Poison of Love
K. R. Meera
Translated by Ministhy S.

'A deep, dark tale'—*The Hindu*
'Enthrallingly disturbing'—*Indian Express*

When Tulsi first meets Madhav, she is irrevocably drawn to his chiselled good looks and charm. Although wary of his many dalliances and the string of broken hearts left in his wake, she is surprised by the intense desire that Madhav arouses in her. And before long, she forsakes her family, her prospective career, her fiancé—all for the love of this inscrutable man.

But love can be like poison. And nothing can prepare Tulsi for the heartache and betrayal that lie ahead.

Years later, Tulsi escapes to the ancient city of Vrindavan, seeking redemption amidst the cries and prayers of its anguished widows. However, when her past catches up with her, old wounds resurface with dramatic consequences.

By turns savage and tender, *The Poison of Love* is a spellbinding tale of love and sacrifice, pain and retribution, confirming K.R. Meera as one of our most fearless and accomplished writers.

ALSO AVAILABLE

Rising Heat

Perumal Murugan

Translated by Janani Kannan

'Unflinchingly honest and poignant'—Firstpost

'A work of understated beauty'—*Mint*

Young Selvan's life is no longer the same. His family's ancestral land has been sold in order to make way for the construction of a housing colony. Now the verdant landscape of his childhood has been denuded, while Selvan and his family are compelled to move to much smaller lodgings. In the ensuing years, as the pressures of their situation simmer to a boil, Selvan observes his family undergo dramatic shifts in their fortunes as greed and jealousy threaten to overshadow their lives. Murugan's first novel, which launched a splendid literary career, is a tour de force. Now translated for the first time, it poses powerful questions about the human cost of relentless urbanization in the name of progress.